J. Azules Amor's
"FUEGO"

EROTIC POETRY, PASSION, AND ROMANCE

J. Azules Amor LLC, Publishing
500 N. Washington Street Unit 1131
Rockville, Maryland 20850 and/or jamor.azules@gmail.com

Ordering Information:
Quantity sales. Special discounts are available on quantity purchases by corporations, associations, and others. For details, contact the publisher at the address above. Orders by U.S. trade bookstores and wholesalers. Please send requests to: jamor.azules@gmail.com

Printed in the United States of America
ISBN 978.1.7358804.7.1
First Edition Print 2021

Front Cover Image illustrated by: Kozakura
Interior Book Design by: Kozakura @ fiverr.com

J. Azules Amor's
"FUEGO"

Foreward

Love is powerful. And from it can betwixt a plethora of emotions. Obviously, it goes beyond love and understanding because love songs, poetry, philosophers have tried to capture its essence since the beginning of time. Too often, sex is treated as taboo and mystical in lieu of the respect it deserves. This book, these poems are about passion, romance, and the in depth energy that sex is; the exchange of souls and energy.

There is no such thing as casual sex. The very essence of sex is spiritual. Anyone who mistakes it for that is fooling themselves into the emptiness that couples itself with the casual mindset.

I hope you enjoy, allow your mind to relax and release and partake of the elixir that is erotic, passionate, and romantic.

-J. Azules Amor

Welcome to les petites morts, a thousand little deaths.

Enjoy.

Table of Contents

Table of Contents cont'd

I Want Your Africa

I want your Africa inside of me
Take me to the Sands of Time until I can get there on my own
BE my hills and valleys and oceans and mountains
and all the vast and wondrous
lands that are the epitome of the Motherland
speak your language in my ear and whisper
all the secrets of the night
let me feel you warmly breathe on my neck as we engage in
skin to skin action
take me to the Serangeti and the start of civilization of all mankind
You can be my dance and my rhythm
and my midnight air
allow me to breathe in your aroma
and taste your skin
Share everything with me
allow me the Vision of blissful skies of pink
and orange magnificent blues and yellows
BE my tribal homeland
because I love looking
into your eyes

your beautiful smile
because beautiful is as close to Heaven as I can get
with my words to tell you how the thoughts of you make me feel
I want you to give me
every drop of the homeland as we connect in orbit
merging your African with my
American and bringing together limitless galaxies
moving through time and space
I love
your voice, your mind, your accent, your humor
and one day I could probably love you too
but for right now put your Africa inside my America
and let's share spirits tonight.

It's Been So Long

It's been so long why are you not here to give me your lovin' ?
To bade my heart by the
sun and moon to induce my body with such worldly pleasures?
My love, mi amor of sweet satisfaction,
do you not hear my heart calling out to you like the wild, wondrous
wolf baying, howling to the moon?
Do you not miss engaging me in our dance of ecstasy
where emotions overrun
and my powers release the passion
as you inject me with your morning elixir?
Oh my love, how sweet it is to partake
in the ethereal pleasures
that you so willingly give
as you rock my body under the sweet, summoning shadows of the
moonlight
and you cast me deeper into your spell of volition?
Oh my sweet love, your
touch brings to me the mystery of sweet seduction
as you convulse me to speak
unknown tongues

as you rhythmically and sweetly take me to foreign lands with your

unfeign touch.

I glide to your rhythm repeatedly, fervently,

giving you all, in that moment,

that I have to give,

expressing my love ceremoniously and unceremoniously

simultaneously ohhhh, mi amor yo necesito todo que tu tiene dar, oh si papi,

es verdadero tu dulce, dulce amor pero dónde cuando el facto es que esta su

amor que

I want so deeply to be wrapped in your love

así que again I ask, why are you not here to

give me your lovin'? It's been so long.

I pray my thoughts whisper upon you

like a

thousand moons

Amen and Ashe

If We Never Speak Again

If we never speak again, I need you to know this.

I really thought of and wanted you to be

the one I shared my soul with.

Maybe it was too deep for you.

Maybe it was too strong for you.

I guess I'll never know.

Never thought it would end like this.

I had real love in my heart

for you and felt a connection.

I believe you felt it too.

Don't know what happened,

but I know I must release you

so that I can go on with my life.

If we never speak again,

I'll miss you.

I miss you now. Everyday I miss you, but if I can't get what I need from you

then

really what's the point?

And I know I haven't asked anything unreasonable.

I haven't asked for your money, only your time.

If we never speak again, know you won't
find many like me, if you find another like me at all.
Remember, I am a butterfly.
But, I just wanted to let you know how I felt and feel about you
in case we never speak again.
It's painful without you.
And although we've known each other for a slight time,
I opened myself up to you and felt you were a very special human being.
I didn't anticipate meeting you,
and I felt, to some extent, we opened up to each other.
So, If we never speak again,
I wish you the best on your journey
and know that I miss you deeply.
I only wanted your time. Quality time.
I'm trying to make sure I express myself as I give myself this closure.
If we never speak again,
Thank you for the smiles and the times you made me feel special to you.
I'm praying
that God will release you from my heart and my consciousness
so that I can be available and
open for the happiness I deserve.
It scared me last week when I realized I had opened my heart to you.
I don't like feeling vulnerable.
And when you changed the way you do things, it made me nervous that
you
would hurt my heart.
My heart, body, or soul hasn't been open to anyone in some years
now.

I was going to tell you that, when we made love,
I was going to tell you to be gentle
with my heart.
I think I have told you everything or most everything.
If we never speak again
know, just know you have made an imprint
on my heart and I owed it to myself
to let you know.

What You Won't Do

What you won't do is have my heart floundering out my chest all on the
ground looking for
a home because you've displaced it after me opening my heart to you.
What you won't do
is having the sweet me coming out of my character having me ready to cut
your ass up
in tiny pieces because you're acting confused all of a sudden as if your
tongue wasn't
really down my throat and swirling in my mouth.
That's what you want do.
What you won't
do is having me question myself and my sanity because now I've either
come out my
character or on the verge of it because you've suddenly gotten a case of
either selective
amnesia or the stupids as if you don't know I care about you or you care
about me.
That's
what you won't do.
Me, having to snap myself out of it because I'm laying in bed or

exercising or writing in my journal or whatever activity
to get you off my mind while playing
Mary J. Blige's 'Share my World' or 'Never Wanna Live Without You'
on repeat while in
my mind's eye I'm talking to you through the song hoping you'll
hear see and feel my
vibrations enough to share your world with me. Nah, you got me confused.
Better yet,
one better. I got me confused that I'm just another broad.
That I'm not special in some
way and that I was confused, delirious, or in some way
misinterpreted your actions and
intentions.
What you won't do is confuse me and allow self doubt to creep in, set itself at
the doorstep of my mind, heart, and soul.
Nah, that's what you won't do!
In the great
words of Spike Lee, 'wake up'!
Having me all confused around here,
going over every
analytical detail, every moment
that we shared in trying to figure out
what went wrong.
Ohhhh no. Oh no. Let me catch myself. Get myself together.
Cause what you won't do is
break myself apart, spinning thoughts and sleepless nights.
Middle of the night crazy.
Yesss, middle of the night crazy.

I take back my power that I had begun to give when I
was starting to open my heart to you and we were starting to open up to
each other.
That's what you won't do.

Milk You

I want to milk you.
I want to squeeze my muscles
and deposit all your gut juice inside of me.
I want your wet, sticky warm thick creamy mix all up inside my guts
as I feel the warm gusts of hot milky pleasure
as you thrust yourself inside of me.
I want to slide down
and glaze your dick with my sweet sauce
and make it look real pretty.
Did I tell you how
much I like singing into your dick anyway?
Yes, I like smelling and sniffing that pretty
thing, that magnificent work of art,
and rubbing that beautiful head
across my warm, wet and wanting lips.

You Make Me So Mad

You make me so mad
I want to fuck you and kill you all at the same time.
You make me so mad.
You make me so damn mad my blood boils.
You can feel the heat emitting from my skin.
I can't sleep
and when I do sleep
I wake up out of it so angry I could curse you
out and strangle yo ass all at the same time
but what I really want is you to fuck me.
I really want to feel your lips on my skin,
your tongue to mine, your taste,
your scent your kiss.
You have awaken something in me
and now there's a stirring that you need to calm
to keep me satisfied.
You've awoken that beast inside and she wants you.
She wants to devour you from inside her thighs.
She wants you to feel the rhythm in her passion as
she rocks these hips and straddles you.

Tick Tock Tick Tock Mothafucka. Yeah, that's
you and you done set it off for round two in this mothafucka.
It's true.
You make me so mad.
You make me so pissed.
In actuality, the piss of pistivity is upon us cause you did this
shyt! I'm gon' own my part in this by opening my heart
but now it's too late for that
because YOU did that shyt with
your kind words and gentlemanly actions.
You gave me a taste of what I've been looking for
and didn't know I needed and now, I want to fuck you
and I need for you to fuck me and give me eternal, ethereal pleasure.
You make me so damn mad!
Now, pick up this damn phone!

Morning Orgasms

I want to wake you up in the mornings and give you head.
I just want to taste it in the
mornings and have you go deep inside my throat.
My biggest decisions some mornings
will be to keep sucking it, to ride it, or sit on your face.
Maybe it will be a morning where I'll
want all three, and then we'll have multiple orgasms together.
You love me so good, and
that makes me want to make you happy,
to bring you joy and continual pleasure.
Your tenderness, kindness, attentiveness, the look in your eyes,
all makes me want to be
submissive to you and give you whatever you want.
I love you with all of me.

I Refuse

I refuse to be bound by the soil in which I was born because
it was the choice where lovers lay
to plant their seed and dreams and passion
being My soul is international
I refrain from being anyone's stereotype
as to what I should learn,
what I should know,
what language I speak
My soul is international
I am a Black woman with a side of Native
American West African Caribbean
Spanish and Portuguese
Iberian Península calling
Ivory Coast calling
pot of gumbo
I accept me
had to solve the mystery as to why I look
like I do
like what I like

born in the states but cook with the Caribbean spice
Bless up
she iré
Me Criss
You Criss
ancestral homelands
Ghana calling my name
porqué yo necesito
hablar qué estás en mi corazón
Why do they try to get me to deny
what's in my blood
and in my soul?
my intuition extends
as my Indigenous roots
of the Cherokee
you see it
when you look at me
born in the states
estadounidense on my certificate
of birth
but my
soul is international

Thank You

Thank you for making me feel safe, protected, and loved.
You care about my tears, my
fears, my joys, my hopes and my dreams.
You show me you care everyday and I truly
appreciate you. The fact that you are comfortable expressing your feelings,
saying what
you want, going for what you want, and being clear and intentional with
your goals is both
loving and sexy.
Thank you for being who you are and praying me into your life.
You are the culmination of my prayers and hopes and whispers and dreams
and I am thankful.
I couldn't have made you better myself if I had a recipe.
You are the epitome of strength
and sensitivity, tenderness and firmness when needed.
I love you and I know in my heart
that I was made for you and you for me.
Thank you mi amor.

The Depths of My Love

I wanna fuck you and slit your throat at the same time.

That's what your love does to me.

Yes, it's terribly violent I know but it's the best way to explain the depths of

my love.

Your love drives me to the edge of insanity. But. Then. I. Stop. And. Catch

myself. And

bring myself back to reality.

But for that brief moment of insanity where I see myself in the

blood and gore of your love, I feel that passion overtake me.

And only God can bring me

back to myself.

Love and Hate

I love you
I want you
I wanna fuck you
I hate your guts.

Serengeti

I want your Africa inside of me
Take me to the Sands of Time
until I can get there on my own
BE my hills and valleys and oceans and mountains and all the vast and wondrous
lands that are the epitome of the Motherland
speak your language in my ear and whisper
all the secrets of the night
let me feel you warmly breath on my neck as we engage in
skin to skin action
take me to the Serengeti and the start of civilization of all mankind
You
can be my dance and my rhythm and my midnight air
allow me to breathe in your aroma
and taste your skin Share everything with me allow me the Vision of blissful
skies of pink
and orange magnificent blues and yellows
BE my tribal homeland
because I love looking
into your eyes your beautiful smile because beautiful is as close to Heaven
as I can get

with my words to tell you how the thoughts of you make me feel
I want you to give me
every drop of the homeland
as we connect in orbit merging your African with my American
and bringing together limitless galaxies moving through time and space
I love your voice, your mind, your accent, your humor and now I love you
too
Our souls connected before we ever knew each other
Because we knew each other in another distant time
With you, time stands still and rotates simultaneously
The Truth is, our souls have been on a yearning search for each other
And I know this is where I am meant to be
This, right now, is our destiny
Our connection on this physical
is just the completion of what was already written
You are my manifest
As I am yours
Souls searching longing from another time
but for right now put your Africa inside my America
and let's share spirits tonight.

Trapped in Paradise

Trapped in Paradise
Island gyurl Island boy no one knows your pain
They don't know your
freedom is confined to the edge of
these beautiful and magnificent turquoise blue jewel
toned waters these planetarium mimicked skies.
They don't know they don't know.
All they think about is their partying, celebrations, vacations
but never in a million years do
their thoughts lend to the limits of your possibilities.
Do they know your happy smiles are
embraced in your imagination?
Imagination of the world beyond those shores where you
will most likely never leave in a lifetime
They don't know
they don't know the expensive
cost and gamble of your dream that may never come to fruition
as they come and go
come and go
What is a passport to you? But they don't hear me though They're too

wrapped up in their partying, celebrations, and vacations to supply any
thought and
energy to your dreams
It has actually never occurred. How often has someone actually
had a conversation with you to see what's behind those eyes and smile?
To know you've never left Paradise and you probably never will
It's enough to bring a tear to your eye
if you go beyond the layer of the island and all the politics
The infinite rests in the finite possibilities
that you may never leave these shores, this island in a lifetime.
This is a salute to the island boy or island gyurl that lives along the majestic
shores
with jeweled toned turquoise waters and planetarium mimicked skies
broken dreams and the infinite
locked in the finite possibilities
as your imagination runs beyond your physical world.
Trapped in Paradise.

Appreciation

Mi amor, I appreciate how you support me in my endeavors.
I appreciate you and want to
please you sexually, while we bring pleasure to each other.
The way you love me and
love on me is so sexy. You never leave me wanting for attention.
When your soft lips
touch mine, you know how to make me cum and bring me to ecstasy.
I want to pleasure you.
I want you in my mouth so that the warm wetness
of the insides of my mouth can
engulf you and taste and feel the lustrous texture of your penis meet
the welcoming
texture of my tongue.
I want to give you pleasure at every stroke and
each time you glide
to meet the back of my throat.
I will erect you to the most delicate of pleasures. On my
knees, for you, as I unleash the pleasure and I want you to look at me, fully,
seeing how I
enjoy you.

Taste my sweet release.
Drink my pleasure and passionately kiss me.
I want to straddle you
as you enter my soul, feel every detail, every inch, and fervent stroke.
I desire all of your warm, sticky goodness.
We will lay with each other and have breakfast
in the morning.
I am here to support your dreams and be what you want and need.
Tell me your secrets
and I'll tell you mine.

Pancakes

I'm hot for you like hot, glazed maple syrup, the pure and dripping on hot
buttered
pancakes.
A fresh stack, hot syrup laden pancakes.
Five stack, freshly made,
maple syrup dripping down the sides of the pancakes and onto the plate,
ready to eat and
devour
And I imagine us
Me dripping my hot honey flavor, buttocks round and taut, as you immerse
your thick,
long, extra stiff energy into my complex inner space.
Our galactic energy as we move
along the stars, my hips rocking to your rhythm.
Can you cum inside and release your Universe inside my welcoming walls,
at just the
right temperature between warm and hot
You slowly and magically disappear inside of me,
as I come closer to your skin, your
body meeting with mine,

and I speak galalah
as you impose yourself into my soul and we
make Mercy together.
I speak in unknown tongues of ecstacy as we exchange spirits in
that spiritual space.
You take me to heights uninamiginable as I imagine me releasing my
Spiritual Essence.
Your God Essence meeting with mine as we worship together in that
spiritual space and
give thanks with the rhythm and song of our bodies

Invoke

I call your name in chant
as if I invoke your Spirit.
The Essence of you and me.
Calling us together. Drawing you closer.
Lighting a candle to represent what we already are.
You manifested me into your life.
Through pain and hardships
our souls have touched
and you are my spiritual journey.
Soon, we will exchange souls
and confirm our evermore.

Yours

Yours is the only cum I want inside of me
Come make love to me in our bed, in our room
I'm waiting for you
Come rock this sweet pussy in the moonlight
Arch my back under the stars
Let me sit on your dick and bounce
and move and stir and grind on it
just the way you like
Move my hips to meet your thrust
your every thrust
Your spirit is in mine
And, I have
given you mine
Our souls are intertwined, and it keeps me with you
It keeps us together
I feel the binding
all of this
Especially when I try to pull away
You know this
You know

I say your name six times and I feel you in me
Our spirits are connected
You call me to you
even when you're far away
And you know, and I know you know

Fucking My Pillow

My ecstacy liqueured stained pillow cases
lingering memories of us
bodies thrusting into each other like that missing
sensation of pressured rotation I needed
as thoughts of you take me
to higher heights of ecstacy
building into a combustible fury
riding my special pillow
imagining it was you
inside of me
on me
me riding you
sucking you, pleasuring you with head
The feeling of you and me together
It's been awhile
And, I need you
Inside me
To elevate my consciousness
to connect me with The Divine
Memories of when that feeling would over come

me, and I would have to stop everything and
listen to my body's rhythm
Pussy liqueur stained pillows that have thirstily
absorbed my sweltering, fervent orgasm
dripping from my lava inner moon
welcoming my every drop
mimicking your cum inside me and dripping out
like fresh, sweet, sticky pineapple juice
clear and sweet
Imagining your giving me what I truly deserve
All of you
inside all of me
seeking that petit mort
my body stiffens to that special death I seek
until my body gives to its release
and then
I sleep

Open Heart

I'll always be thankful
I'll always be grateful
for the love we shared
You opened my heart
One which was closed off for love
And you did that for me
I took a chance
To find romance
And romance seeked me
And found me Again
For you my evermore
And I your Omalicha
Mi Obi Mu
My amorous heart
My heart is open to you
As we move on
Amongst the magic dust of love
Always feeling safe in your arms
Hearing your heartbeat
Our rhymthic breathing in harmony

Beyond the arguments
And naysayers
You remain my Forever Love
And I your Wahala Woman
The Passion they may never understand
For all its real for all its true
I flew over continents to be in your arms
That sacred space I yearned to be
I loved you then
I love you now

Taste My Delight

Taste my delight
Place your tongue on my pink pearl
and suck it 'til my juices flow
Put your tongue in my milky way galaxy
and inhale my aroma
Smother yourself in my pineapple and mango delight
My erect nipples welcome your touch
Kiss me and allow me to taste myself
Make my body your musical instrument
as I wet your face with pleasure
My backdoor galaxy awaits to be explored by your tongue
The smoothness of my fresh sugar preparation
allows you to taste me with no interruption
Put your finger in my backdoor
and devour me
while you drink my yummy goodness
Bring me to that ecliptic, mesmeric, climactic
volcanic eruption
As your mouth meets my private spot
and I cradle you between my thighs
Take me until there is no more
Satisfy your appetite until I have no more left to give
The laundry can wait 'til morning

Fantasy

Allow me to be your fantasy
And I'll dress up the way you want me to
Tonight I don't want you to pull my hair
And I don't want you to choke me
I can crawl to you and you make me
beg for it
or I can be your bytch and you can be
my pimp
I'll call you Big Daddy and you can
tell me what to do
or we can leave the drapes open and allow
the neighbors to watch
I can dress in my sheer black stockings
the ones with the line in the back
put on my highest heels
and obey your every command
Allow me to be your fantasy
We can be whoever we want to be
Release our inhibitions
As we enter the pleasure zone

You don't need to spank me tonight
unless you want to
Allow me to be your fantasy
Your wish is my command

Dear Love

Dear Love,
I feel so lost without you. And I'm wondering how I can
love somebody this much?
My world is not the same without you. My life will never be the same.
Our souls
have touched on different planes, and I realize I cannot live without you.
I can never
unmeet the person I loved and love and found in you.
Being without you is torture. I thought I could do it on my own,
learn to live without you.
But I'm happier with you than without you. And although you
drive me crazy at times,
and I know I do the same, I'd rather face the world with you
than without you.
Facing the reality that my life will never be the same.

A Dream

You kissed me and made me cum

It was so magical, the way you brought me to ecstacy

and I look forward to us doing that again

I want to pleasure you. I look forward to pleasuring you and

having you in my mouth

I want the warm wetness of the insides of my mouth to engulf you

I want to taste you and have the lustrous texture of your penis meet the

welcoming

texture of my tongue

I want to give you pleasure at every stroke and each time you glide to meet

the back of my throat

I look forward to waking you up in the mornings with my mouth on your

love mound

erecting you to the most delicate of pleasures

I'm on my knees while I unleash the pleasures that I give you

I want you to see how much I enjoy you

I'll be glad for you to suck on my clit and taste and swallow my juices

I want to give you that sweet release as I release on your tongue and in

your mouth. Drink my pleasure. I want you to enter me as you are deeply and

passionately kissing me simultaneously. You're making me cum

We will lay with each other and have breakfast afterwards.
Maybe we'll make love again
whereas this time I'm riding you. I straddle you as you
gently enter my soul. I want to feel
every inch of you, every detail. I want you to guide my hips as you
center me on that
perfect spot and I'll cum over and over again.
I want you to witness and feel my
pleasure. Eventually, we get to the point
where you're taking me from the back
holding on to me and pulling me closer to you
as you give me long, deep thrusts
and fervent strokes of your beautiful love muscle.
I'm going to love it when we cum
together and you unload all of your love juice inside of me.
I so look forward to that
warm, sticky goodness

Tell Me

If you miss me, tell me so
Speak my name upon your lips
The essence of nectar
that sounds so sweet
Tell me what I mean to you
and that I'm your one and only

Tell me of your love divine
and refrain from sending me
in these streets lonely
lest not hold your feelings from me
Trust. Your feelings are safe with me
Your secrets are my secrets
Your concerns are my concerns

love's reciprocity
we can cry together
share the beauty of love
If you miss me, tell me so
speak my name upon your lips

Drug

My love is so deep for you that it scares me.
When I sit here and think about it, meditate on it,
and think you've become like a drug, and when
I close my eyes I can feel you coursing through
my veins.
I can feel you, even when you're not here.
I try to let go. I can't. The most I've been able to do
is a few days at a time.
It's like some kind of unhealthy type of love. It's like
being happy and miserable all at the same time.
And I almost can't function when you're not here,
And I don't like the Power you have over me.

You and Me

You and Me
That's all there needs to Be
As the Universe unfolds
inside of me
The depths of my heart
The yearning of my mind
Articulated Passion
Curated Action
I see you in me
And I hold the strings to your heart
you can't get me out of your mind
No matter how hard you try
And I in sleepless nights of midnight
you and me as the Passion unfolds
because you are my great big Universe
and I am Yours
Time and Distance are only culprits
Souls speak stronger than any remnant
of understanding
That's why sleepless nights

trail us to the Universe
gold and blue and flecks of time
that don't make sense
but not meant to
Everything is not to be understood
be with you if I could
I love you
And no matter how far away
My heart is with you
and yours with mine
They won't understand it
or understand us
When it's all said and done
The Universe speaks
you and me
there is no greater love
because we represent it
I am thankful for my God essence
as the Universe unfolds
we've been together before
Before we ever met
our souls touched
and recognized each other
you are that yearning
And I need you
it's not for us to understand
nor us fully
It is the Passion of the Universe

as it unfolds
Transcending time and space
blue lights of forever gold
My heart is with you
and in your hands

Fastidious

I love you like the honeysuckle rose and Heaven
rolled up all in one
I'd taste your sweat right now if I could
and delight in the delectable sweetness of
its salty tone.
I'd urgently take you into my body
as you lose yourself in the
Seven Wonders of My Love
You'd dance in fantasy dipthong
Essence of ecstacy
and moonlight delight where reality meets
with the planes of non existence
and worlds merge in fastidious passion

Acknowledgement

Thank you for being an inspiration to write poetry.

The original poet,
Auntie Maxine "Dimples" Brown.